Nella
THE
PRINCESS
KNIGHT

W9-BYY-127

Follow Your NOSE!

A Scratch-and-Sniff Adventure

Illustrated by Jason Fruchter

Random House 🏠 New York

rhcbooks.com
ISBN 978-0-525-57792-8
MANUFACTURED IN CHINA
10 9 8 7 6 5 4 3 2 1

Nella and her friends were excited to be at the Castlehaven County Fair . . . except for Willow. She was feeling shy because she'd never been to a fair before.

"Just give it a try," Nella said, taking Willow by the hand. She showed her all the fresh fruits and sweet-smelling treats. Sir Garrett loved the peach pies!

Willow entered a tent filled with fragrant flowers.
"What is this place?" she asked.
"It's where the Castlehaven County Fair Gardening Contest is held," Nella said.

Clod showed everyone the blue pennant the champion would win—but then he slipped and fell onto a small tree, snapping its trunk!

"That's okay," Willow said. "I can help."

She knew an old gardening trick.
She sprinkled the tree with a potion
and said some magic words:

*"Pat a little dirt. Let the potion flow.
Stomp, clap, turn. Now grow, plant, grow!"*

The tree sprang back to life! The
trunk was fixed, and the leaves were
fresher than ever.
    "Girl, you're a gardening superstar!"
Trinket exclaimed.
    "Willow, you should enter
the gardening contest!"
Nella suggested.

Willow was nervous, but she decided to give the contest a try. She planted a watermelon seed and used every gardening trick she knew. She may have used too many. . . .

The watermelon grew and grew until it burst through the tent! Its vines wrapped around the bakers, Uta and Ida.

Nella knew this was a job for a Princess Knight!

Nella transformed into a Princess Knight and ran to the rescue. First she untangled Uta and Ida. Then she shot a ribbon arrow into a tall pile of hay bales and pulled the bakers to safety.

The watermelon kept growing and growing.
It even knocked over the lemonade stand!
"No, no, no!" cried Willow. "My watermelon is
ruining everything!"

"Enough is enough," said Nella. "We've got to get rid of that watermelon!"

"Listen up, everyone," Nella announced. "I've got a plan to catapult that watermelon right out of here!"

She shoved her lance under the melon. Then she and her friends jumped on the lance's handle. All their weight caused the melon to spring into the air and fly toward the hills outside Castlehaven.

Oh, no! The giant watermelon started rolling back toward town! Willow had an idea.

She quickly grew some purple trees. The watermelon bounced off them and sailed over Castlehaven. The town and the fair were saved!

The watermelon finally landed—on the edge of the castle's moat. It cracked open and filled with water. Nella's friends spent the rest of the day splashing and playing in the new pool!

Trinket made sure to put on sunscreen.
"Best Castlehaven County Fair ever!" she
shouted as she jumped into the water.

Willow thanked Nella for a wonderful day. "I never thought I'd save a kingdom from a giant rolling watermelon," she said.

"You never know what you can do unless you try!" said Nella.